THE PUPPY PLACE

BARNEY

THE PUPPY PLACE

Don't miss any of these other stories by Ellen Miles!

Angel

Bandit

Baxter

Bear

Bella

Bentley

Bitsy

Bonita

Boomer

Bubbles and Boo

Buddy

Champ

Chewy and Chica

Cocoa

Cody

Cooper

Cuddles

Daisy

Edward

Flash

Gizmo

Goldie

Gus

Honey

Jack

Jake

Kodiak

Liberty

Lola

Louie

Lucky

Lucy

Maggie and Max

Mocha

Molly

Moose

Muttley

Nala

Noodle

Oscar

Patches

Princess

Pugsley

Rascal

Rocky

Roxy

Rusty

Scout

Shadow

Snowball

Spirit

Stella

Sugar, Gummi, and Lollipop

Sweetie

Teddy

Ziggy

Zipper

THE PUPPY PLACE

BARNEY

ELLEN
MILES

SCHOLASTIC INC.

ISBN 978-1-338-57218-6

10 9 8 7 6 5 4 3   20 21 22 23 24

Printed in the U.S.A.   40
First printing 2020

CHAPTER ONE

Lizzie rubbed her hands together. She blew on her fingertips, but her hands were still stiff and cold. She'd been silly to leave her gloves at home, but at least they wouldn't be covered in mud like everything else she was wearing.

"If you're cold, you can put your hands on Picadilly's neck," Maria said. "Dilly is super warm." Maria was Lizzie's best friend and Picadilly was the pony Maria rode in lessons and horse shows. Everyone called him "Dilly" for short.

"Thanks for inviting me to your horse show," Lizzie said to Maria as she buried her hands in Dilly's thick mane. Maria was right. The pony's warmth made Lizzie's fingers tingle as the cold left them.

"It's great to have you here," Maria said.

Maria was in the saddle, getting ready to compete. She leaned forward and wrapped her arms around the pony's neck. She buried her face in his thick, gray mane, closed her eyes, and let out a happy sigh.

Lizzie smiled. Maria loved horses the way she, Lizzie, loved dogs.

And Lizzie *really* loved dogs. Especially her own puppy, Buddy. He was sweet and playful and loyal. He was the best. Of all the puppies her family had fostered over the years, he was the only one they'd kept forever. By now, Lizzie and her younger brothers, Charles and the Bean, felt like Buddy was another sibling.

"Dilly and I are in the next class," Maria said.

"Could you grab the cloth out of the brush box and wipe that mud off his face?"

Lizzie bent down and picked a brown rag out of the wooden box at her feet.

"Whoops! Not that one. That's my boot rag," Maria said to Lizzie. "The blue one is for Dilly's face. Because he's a blue-ribbon pony."

Lizzie nodded. She knew that Maria and Dilly had not won a blue ribbon—yet! Maria had just started showing. She had already won one red ribbon for second place, which was pretty good for a newbie.

Lizzie found a clean part of the blue cloth. She ran it over the white swirl in the center of Dilly's face. She looked into the pony's deep, dark eyes, and he gazed back at her. He was so calm and gentle.

"It's really a big help having you here," Maria said.

"It's fun," Lizzie said. She used the rag to polish a silver buckle on Dilly's bridle. "And I haven't even seen you ride yet today."

"Well, you will soon," Maria said. "Our first class is about to begin." She took a deep breath and patted Dilly's neck. "Wake up, boy." Maria sat up straight and tightened her reins.

Lizzie looked around. The horse show was a busy place. There were trucks and trailers parked all along the riding club's driveway. Inside a big white barn, there were rows of stalls and a big indoor riding ring. Today, all the classes were taking place outside. The outdoor rings, each with a wood fence, were in a large, grassy field.

Kathy, Maria's riding trainer, walked up to them. "Hey, Lizzie," Kathy said. "It's nice of you to help Maria out." Kathy ran her hand down Dilly's neck, and the pony snorted and pushed his nose against her arm.

Lizzie had met Kathy before. When Maria had talked Lizzie into taking riding lessons, Kathy had been her trainer. Thanks to Kathy, Lizzie wasn't nervous around horses anymore.

"What do you think of your first horse show?" Kathy asked.

Lizzie smiled. "It's great," she said. "I can't believe how many horses are here. There are horses everywhere."

At Kathy's barn, most of the horses were in stalls. It was very different at the show. Some horses stood tied next to trailers. Other horses jumped fences in another ring by the big barn. Horses and riders waited in groups by the show ring for their next class. All the horses were gleaming, their coats newly groomed. Tails swished. Ears twitched. Hooves stamped. Lizzie was very glad that she'd gotten over her fear of horses.

"There is a lot going on," Kathy agreed. "It's

good that Dilly is so mellow and cool." She scratched under the pony's chin. "He's the calmest pony I've ever known."

"He's the best," Maria agreed, leaning down to put her arms around Dilly's neck again.

Kathy gave Maria some final pointers, and then Maria and Dilly entered the ring. Lots of other horse-and-rider teams went in, too.

Lizzie grabbed the brush box and went to watch at the fence. Maria had told Lizzie about this class. All the horses and riders went into the ring together. They would walk, trot, and canter. Then they would change direction and do it all again.

An intercom crackled. "Class eight, ages thirteen and younger, it's time to begin," a man announced. "Please walk. All walk."

Lizzie was nervous for Maria. She gripped the top rail of the fence and watched. It was easy to find Picadilly. He was the only dappled gray pony in the ring.

"Trot, all trot," the voice said. The horses and ponies sped up to a trot.

Lizzie bit her lip as Maria and Picadilly passed. Maria didn't turn toward Lizzie. She looked straight ahead, concentrating hard. The horses and ponies all seemed to move together. Lizzie sensed a rhythm: the creaking of saddles, the soft snorts, the even thuds of the hooves on the ground.

Then a dog's loud, shrill bark rang out. There was another bark, even louder, followed by a long outpouring of high-pitched yelping that echoed off the barn.

"Barney, no!" a voice cried. "Barney, come back!"

Lizzie saw a flash of motion across the ring, followed by more barking.

The even rhythm of the show ring vanished. Bridles jangled as horses threw up their heads. Their high, frightened whinnies filled the air. Horses and ponies darted in different directions as their riders tried to hold on. Lizzie could feel their thudding hoofbeats in her body, matching the sudden beating of her own heart.

It took Lizzie a moment to figure out what was happening.

Then she spotted a puppy in the ring, a copper-colored puppy with short legs and a long body. He was fast! His front legs flew out in front of him as he dashed here and there across the grassy ring. It was hard to believe that just one puppy was making all that noise! One small puppy, with bright eyes, wild eyebrows, and a long, scruffy beard. The little guy was barking at—and chasing!—every horse he saw.

CHAPTER TWO

The puppy ran in big circles, barking madly. Horses pranced in place. Ponies dashed this way and that. Some of the riders looked terrified, and Lizzie could tell that they did not know what to do. She would have been terrified, too.

Lizzie wanted to run into the ring and grab the puppy, but she hesitated. She knew a lot about dogs, but she didn't know that much about horses. What happened if one of the horses was scared? What if it reared up, or ran right at her? Would she get kicked, or trampled? Even one of the smaller ponies could hurt her badly.

"Halt! Everyone stop," came a man's voice over

the loudspeaker. "Halt your horses." The voice paused. The loudspeaker crackled again as all the riders pulled on their reins, asking the horses to stop. "Can someone please get this adorable puppy out of the ring?"

"Coming!" a voice called out. "Barney! Here, boy!"

Lizzie looked across the ring and saw a woman leaning over the fence. She was the one calling the dog. The woman was holding a little girl, about the same age as Lizzie's younger brother the Bean.

Now Lizzie knew what she could do to help. She took off. The brush box clanged against her leg as she ran toward the woman and the girl. "Excuse me, excuse me," she mumbled as she threaded her way through the crowd.

"Baa-nee!" the little girl called in a tiny voice. She waved at the mischievous puppy. "Baa-nee, come!"

"Barney!" yelled the woman.

Maybe Barney did not hear the woman and the little girl—or maybe Barney was ignoring them. The bossy little pup seemed to want to order all the horses around. He wrinkled his nose as he barked, and his tail wagged at superspeed.

Look at these gigantic animals with their silly extra-long legs! They are everywhere! I must alert everyone.

"Barney!" the woman yelled again.

"I can help," Lizzie said when she reached the woman and the girl. "I can watch your little girl so you can go in the ring."

The woman frowned as she looked Lizzie up and down. She pressed her lips together, thinking.

"I have a little brother who's about her age," Lizzie said. Her brother, the Bean, was always getting into mischief—but she knew how to handle him. "I take care of him all the time."

Just then, the loudspeaker crackled again.

"Okay," the woman said. She drew in a deep breath. "Fine. I'm Polly, and this is Cassie. Cassie," she began, turning to the girl, "Mama is going to go get Barney. You stay here with—"

"Lizzie," Lizzie said quickly, and she leaned down so she could look Cassie in the eye. "I'm Lizzie. Mama is going to bring Barney back so he is nice and safe."

"Mama," Cassie whined, watching her mother climb into the ring.

"We're going to wait right here for Mama," Lizzie said. "Here, look at all these special brushes for taking care of horses." She sat down with Cassie and opened the brush box, hoping to distract the little girl. That usually worked with the Bean.

On the other side of the ring, Barney was on

the run. The puppy ran right up to a tall black horse and barked. The horse tossed its head in the air. A shrill whinny rang out as it stamped a front hoof just as Barney dodged away.

Barney bounded off and then ran back. He got down on his haunches, wagged his tail, and let out another bunch of high-pitched yelps.

Do I want to play with them? I'm not even sure myself, to be honest.

"Wirehaired dachshund," a man said.

Lizzie turned in surprise. That was exactly what she had been thinking. Whenever Lizzie saw a dog, she loved to try to guess its breed, and usually she was right. With its long body and short legs, this puppy did look like a dachshund. Instead of a short, smooth coat, this one had slightly longer fur that looked thick, like the bristles on a paintbrush. The puppy's coat was a beautiful caramel color, golden brown. He was far away, but Lizzie could tell he had a mischievous sparkle in his eyes. His wild, wiry eyebrows and the bouncy way he moved made him look almost like a cartoon character.

The man next to Lizzie had pretty wild eyebrows himself, along with snow-white hair and a well-trimmed beard. He sat in a folding chair by the fence, right next to where Polly and Cassie's blanket was spread on the ground. The man stared into the ring, pointing at Barney. "There are plenty of dog breeds that are good around horses, but the dachshund is not one of them. No sir."

Lizzie wasn't sure what to say, or even if she was supposed to say anything. She stroked Cassie's arm, trying to keep her calm. But the little girl was restless. She squirmed her way out of Lizzie's lap. "Here, I'll pick you up," Lizzie offered, but the toddler pushed her away.

"They're coming back in just a minute," Lizzie said again. She held on to the little girl's hood to make sure she didn't escape. Cassie was even more stubborn than the Bean. Maybe it would have been better if she'd gone into the ring to rescue Barney, after all.

When Lizzie looked back into the ring, Barney was still chasing the horses. He raced after one, then leapt away and chased another. He bounded around the horses' flying hooves. He was having a fine time. Polly, Cassie's mother, was not. Every time Polly came close to Barney, he would bolt away, dashing to the other side of a horse or hiding behind a jump. Polly kept trying to grab his leash, and kept missing.

Out of the corner of her eye, Lizzie could see the grumpy man shake his head. "It's just not right," he mumbled.

"Hal Bixby, do you need to share *all* your opinions?" A woman sat down next to him. She placed a travel mug in his cup holder and patted him on the back. "I think it's sweet that he's here," the woman said. Lizzie guessed that she must be Mrs. Bixby. "Dogs like to be part of a family." She took a sip from her own mug. "All dogs. Dachshunds included."

"But dachshunds aren't always—"

"—good with small kids," the woman finished the man's sentence. "I know, I know. It's true."

Mr. Bixby nodded and sighed. Then he said, "Small kids will try—"

"—to pick them up." The woman finished his sentence again. "And that isn't good. I know. You're absolutely right."

"It's just not safe," the man added. "Not good for the dog."

Did the man want Lizzie to hear what they were saying? Lizzie wanted to tell him that Barney wasn't her dog—and Cassie wasn't her sister—but he was so grouchy. She didn't dare look his way. She wished he would mind his own business. She had enough to worry about. When Lizzie looked back down, Cassie had climbed half-way into the ring!

CHAPTER THREE

"Baa-nee!" Cassie yelled. She clapped her hands. "Baa-nee!" She began to jump up and down, making her wispy pigtails bounce up and down along with her.

Lizzie ran to catch Cassie and bring her back behind the fence. "Cassie, we have to wait here for Mama," she said once they were safely back.

"But I want Baa-nee!" Cassie sobbed, pointing. "What if that horse hurts him?"

Lizzie followed the little girl's gaze. She saw Barney, barking his head off as he stood his ground in the middle of the ring. Then Lizzie saw that Maria had gotten off Picadilly. She was leading the gray pony by his reins, and they were both walking toward Barney. The puppy's whole body shook as he barked at Maria and Picadilly.

Lizzie watched as Maria moved toward the dog, step by slow step. Picadilly followed her, his head relaxed and low. The pony didn't even flick an ear at the puppy's antics. "It's okay," Lizzie whispered to Cassie. "My friend Maria looks like she knows what she's doing. I think her pony Picadilly is used to dogs."

Barney could not have barked any louder. His tail could not have wagged any harder. He watched the pony and girl approach.

Yay, here they come! Maybe we can play. Or maybe I need to protect my humans from them. I'll just keep barking, in any case.

Lizzie held her breath. She watched as Maria bent over to whisper to the peppy little dog. Lizzie could not hear what Maria was saying, but the puppy stopped barking for two seconds. That was when Maria reached slowly out and grabbed his leash. Lizzie felt like cheering. Maria had caught the mischievous pup. The sudden silence was wonderful after all that barking.

Polly looked grateful as she hurried over to Maria. She scooped Barney up. The puppy wriggled and squirmed as Polly carried him across the ring, cradling him as if he were a little baby.

Lizzie gave Maria a big thumbs-up. Her best friend had saved the day.

"Now, see? That woman is carrying the dachshund correctly," Mr. Bixby pointed out.

"Mama!" Cassie cried as Polly slipped back through the fence.

Cassie threw herself against her mother's legs.

Polly settled Barney onto the ground and handed his leash to Lizzie so she could hug her daughter. Cassie clung to her mother's knees, and Barney whimpered, jumping up at the little girl's back.

"Down, Barney. It's okay, Cassie." Polly sighed as she rubbed Cassie's back. "What am I going to do with you two?" she asked.

"He's a handful, isn't he?" Lizzie asked.

Polly smiled, shaking her head. "He sure is," she said. "My brother meant well when he surprised us with the gift of this little pup, but—" She blew a puff of air up so her bangs flew into the air. "Phew. What can I say? It's been a little hectic in our house ever since he arrived. Cassie can't seem to leave Barney alone, and Barney can't seem to settle down."

The action in the ring started back up, but Lizzie almost forgot to watch the rest of Maria's class as she and Polly talked. Lizzie found out that Cassie had an older sister named Mavis, and that both girls adored Barney. "But these days Mavis spends too much time at the riding stable to help out much, and Cassie is too young to help. She tries, but she probably makes more messes than she cleans up."

Lizzie's family had fostered a lot of puppies. She remembered how hard it was for the Bean when her family first started taking in dogs who needed temporary homes. He'd had to be taught not to pet and hug them when they were too tired or not in the mood. Lizzie knew that toddlers and pup-pies were not always a good mix.

"I really love Barney, but my hands were already full with my girls before he showed up," Polly said. She scratched Barney under the chin. Cassie reached out to pet Barney but ended up poking him in the belly instead. "Gentle, Cassie,"

Polly directed. "Remember, nice and gentle with Barney."

Cassie leaned toward Barney and grabbed him around the belly with both hands. She stood up and tried to walk off with the little dog. Barney wriggled and whimpered. Lizzie could see the whites of his eyes; he looked scared.

Put me down!

"Cassie, no!" Polly ran after her to take the puppy away. "Do I need a leash for you, too?"

Lizzie noticed that Mr. and Mrs. Bixby were watching the whole thing. Mr. Bixby was scowling, but Mrs. Bixby's gaze was kind.

Maria's class was still going on. Lizzie looked into the ring to see that the horses and ponies were going around in big circles. Lizzie caught

Maria's eye and smiled encouragingly, giving her friend a tiny wave.

"No, Barney!" Lizzie turned to see Polly reaching for the puppy's collar. "No digging."

Barney was pawing wildly at the ground. He had chunks of mud and grass in his paws. He got in two more good swipes at his hole before Polly pulled him away.

Polly had one arm around Cassie. She tugged at Barney's leash with the other. She didn't ask for help, but Lizzie could tell she needed it.

"Come on, boy," Lizzie said in a soft voice. Carefully, she picked Barney up and pulled him into her lap. The puppy whined and struggled to get away. His paws left muddy smears all over Lizzie's jeans. Lizzie didn't care. She scratched Barney under the chin and her fingers found their way past his long coarse hair to the softer coat underneath. Slowly, Barney started to relax. "It just takes time," Lizzie whispered to him. "Right? You just need a little time to get all that energy out and settle down."

Lizzie had been talking to Barney, but Polly responded. "Sadly, time is something I just don't have," she said with a sigh. "I really wish I did."

"And the winner of the blue ribbon for this class," Lizzie heard the announcer say, "is Maria Santiago, riding Picadilly."

Lizzie looked into the ring just in time to see a woman reaching up to pin a big blue ribbon onto Picadilly's bridle. Maria had won first place!

"I have to go," Lizzie said, grabbing the brush box. "Cassie, I had fun with you. I hope I see you again." Barney looked up at her and wagged his tail, an innocent expression on his face. "Little troublemaker," Lizzie whispered as she gave him a good-bye pat. He really was adorable. But she had to hurry if she wanted to meet Maria when she came out of the ring.

"You won!" Lizzie greeted her best friend. She patted Picadilly on his neck and smiled up at Maria.

"I know! I can't believe it," Maria said, grinning. "I mean, who knows? Maybe I only won because I caught that pesky little puppy."

"Well, you deserve a blue ribbon just for that," Lizzie said. "It was brave."

"I knew Dilly would be fine," said Maria. "He never shies away from loud sounds, and he's used to dogs. He's good that way." Maria jumped down from the saddle and hugged the pony's neck. "Thanks, boy. You were a star."

Lizzie admired the shiny blue satin ribbon in Maria's hand. "Very fancy."

"Maria!" Kathy called out. The horse trainer

rushed over to give Maria a high five. "You and Dilly were amazing. You saved Barney, and you won the class."

Lizzie looked from Kathy to Maria. "Wait, you already knew Barney?" Lizzie asked.

"Sure. We've met him at the stable," said Maria. "I don't think Mavis's family really wanted a dog, but I know that Barney was a present for Mavis and her little sister."

"I heard about that," Lizzie said. Kathy and Maria looked at her. "I mean, I met Mavis's mom," Lizzie went on. "I watched Cassie so Polly could get Barney out of the ring. Then I helped to calm Barney down while I talked with them for a while."

Maria smiled and shook her head. "This may be a horse show, but you are Lizzie Peterson," Maria said. "You always find a dog, wherever you go."

CHAPTER FOUR

Lizzie smiled back. Maria was right. Lizzie *did* find dogs everywhere. She couldn't help it. She loved dogs.

But today wasn't about dogs. It was about Maria, and ponies and horses. Lizzie wanted to be a good best friend. It was why she was there. Lizzie knew what she had to do. She had to forget about Barney and focus on Maria—and Dilly— for the rest of the day.

"I'm so glad I came," Lizzie said as Maria clipped Dilly's lead to Kathy's trailer.

"I'm super glad, too," Maria said. "Especially

since my dad couldn't stay. Oh, and Kathy said we can get the apples for your World Food Fair project on the way back home later on."

"That's perfect," Lizzie said. "I saw lots of apples on display at that farm stand we passed on the way here."

Later that week, Lizzie and Maria's grade would be hosting a World Food Fair for the whole school. Students had to bring in a food to share, something that represented a family tradition. Lizzie had decided to bring in apple butter, which she'd learned to make with her aunt Amanda. Lizzie loved peanut butter and apple butter sandwiches. They tasted like home.

Maria patted Dilly's neck after she and Lizzie had brushed him down. "You get some rest, boy. We still have a big day ahead." Maria's next class was in the afternoon, so they had a long break.

Maria turned to Lizzie. "My dad gave me money for the food truck," she said with a smile. "Ready for lunch?"

Lizzie and Maria found the food truck by the barn. Maria ordered a hamburger, Lizzie chose grilled cheese, and they both got hot chocolate, just to warm themselves up. They sat at a nearby picnic table. Maria had grabbed an extra horse blanket from the trailer, and she draped it over their shoulders as they huddled together for warmth.

"I should have come to a show over the summer," Lizzie said. She was shivering, even with her winter coat zipped up all the way.

"Summer shows are fun," Maria said, wrapping her hands around her cup of hot chocolate. "But a lot of them are far away. This stable is so close. Kathy's barn is only, like, five minutes from here. She's good friends with this barn's trainers."

Lizzie nodded. "That's cool."

"Since you're here," Maria said, "maybe you can help me memorize the courses for the jumping classes I'm doing later? Dad usually helps me do it."

"Sure. Sounds fun," Lizzie replied.

"It's so much easier with two people," Maria said. "You just have to quiz me."

As they ate, Lizzie looked at a cue card with a picture of the fences in the show ring. There were numbers by the fences, one to eight. Maria went over the order of the jumps again and again. Maria knew all the names for the fences—like the oxer or the in-and-out—and she knew how many strides Dilly should take between each jump.

"It's a lot to remember," Lizzie said.

"I know, right?" Maria agreed.

"I don't think I could memorize them all," Lizzie admitted.

"Um, yeah, you could," Maria said. "You memorized your entire 'Dog Breeds of the World' poster." Then she went back to reciting the three courses by heart.

Three dogs trotted by at the heel of a woman in knee-high green rubber boots. The dogs playfully nipped at one another's short tails. *Two Welsh corgis and a Jack Russell*, thought Lizzie as her eyes wandered from the course cue cards to the dogs.

"Wait," Maria said, shaking her head. "Did I just mess up?"

Lizzie looked back down at the card in her hand. "I don't think so," she said, though she wasn't at all sure.

"Lizzie!" Maria said. "You were watching those dogs." She laughed out loud. Maria knew her best friend too well.

"You're right. I'm so sorry." Lizzie said. "I was just thinking about how corgis and Jack Russell terriers are good horse dogs, and then I wondered why Barney doesn't seem like a horse dog at all."

"You really have a one-track mind," Maria said. "That's what my mom would say."

"That *is* what my mom says," Lizzie said, and they both laughed. Lizzie knew she was lucky to have a friend who knew her so well.

After a while, Lizzie decided to say what was really on her mind. "I can tell how much Polly and Cassie love Barney," Lizzie began, but then she paused. She bit her lip. She felt bad to even say it out loud. "And I'm sure Mavis does, too. But—"

"But?" Maria prompted.

"But I think Barney might be too much puppy for that family." There. It was out. Lizzie didn't feel any better, but she still believed it was true.

"Are you saying what I think you're saying?" Maria asked.

"I am," Lizzie replied. "He's too much for them, and they're too much for him. I can tell that he doesn't like the way Cassie grabs him. I think that family needs some help with Barney."

CHAPTER FIVE

The jumping was so exciting that Lizzie held her breath as she watched. She loved watching the horses fly over the jumps, the riders perfectly in sync with their moves. Maria remembered the courses perfectly for her jumping classes. By the time the horse show ended, Maria and Picadilly really had something to celebrate. they were reserve champion for their division, which Lizzie learned was like second place overall. Lizzie was so proud of her best friend—and her best friend's pony! She gave Dilly a big hug before Maria and Kathy loaded him into Kathy's trailer.

"Hi, Lizzie?"

"Oh—hi, Polly," Lizzie said. She'd been so involved in the jumping event that she'd almost forgotten about the Barney problem. Polly had Cassie propped on her hip, and she had Barney on a very tight leash.

"I just wanted to thank you again for watching Cassie," Polly said. She shifted so the little girl was higher on her hip.

"I was happy to help," Lizzie said. "I'm glad you got Barney back safe and sound." Lizzie smiled down at the puppy. He looked up and seemed to smile back at her, working his funny, shaggy eyebrows up and down. He tilted his head, gazing at her with his sparkly eyes.

"I'm glad, too," Polly said. "Um, listen. After Barney got loose, I spoke to Kathy. She told me your family fosters puppies. We're about to go away on a trip, and we could use a break while we get ready for it. I wonder if you could help us out."

"Um," Lizzie wasn't sure what to say. It was exactly what she'd been thinking earlier: That Polly and her family could use some time off from Barney. But did Polly want to give him up for good, or just for a few days?

"Kathy gave me your mom's number and I was about to call her to speak about you taking Barney from us for a while," Polly went on. "But I wanted to ask what you think about it. I mean, I'm starting to think that Barney might be a bit much for our family right now. Maybe we even have to think about giving him up for good."

Lizzie saw Cassie's face fall. She could tell that the little girl was about to start wailing. "Well, I think—"

"Mom! No!" A teenager walked up. She was wearing a green down jacket over her show coat.

She looked a lot like Cassie, without the bright-pink baby cheeks and pigtails. Lizzie figured she must be Mavis, Cassie's big sister.

"Don't say that in front of Cassie," Mavis insisted, squeezing her sister's shoulder. "It isn't fair. She loves Barney. We all do." Mavis bent down to pet Barney. "Good boy," she said as Barney barked and spun in circles.

Polly sighed. "It'll just be a trial run," she said to Mavis. "I think Barney needs a break from us as much as we need one from him."

"But how can you say good-bye to those big eyes and bushy eyebrows? Are you sure, Mom?" Mavis asked.

"I am," Polly said. "I've been thinking about this for a while. I love Barney—we all do—but he's just too full of energy." She smiled sadly at the feisty little pup by her side.

"Baa-nee!" Cassie squealed. She reached her

little arms around Barney's belly. Barney put his tail between his legs and flashed Lizzie a frightened look.

"Uh-uh! No picking up Barney," Polly told Cassie. She paused and then looked up at Lizzie. "I have to remind her of that about eighty times a day," she said, sighing. She petted Barney again. "He's a good dog, he really is. He just complicates our already complicated life."

Lizzie felt the worst for Cassie. It was clear how much the little girl loved the puppy—but if the two of them weren't separated soon, who knew what might happen? So far, Barney just tried to get away from her when she grabbed him, but Lizzie knew that some dachshunds had a reputation for being nippy.

An hour later, Lizzie and Maria were at the farm stand—with Barney—picking out apples.

Lizzie could hardly believe it was still the same day. So much had happened! Polly and Lizzie had each talked to Lizzie's mom, and it hadn't taken long for them to agree that the Petersons would watch Barney while Polly's family got ready for their trip.

Lizzie looked over the baskets of apples, biting her thumb. The farm stand had all kinds of apples—green with shiny skin, red with green patches, pale green with freckles, bright red, pinkish red. She didn't know which ones to choose. And Lizzie couldn't forget to buy a box of a dozen apple-cider doughnuts, too. She'd promised Charles she would bring some home.

Lizzie looked around, but there wasn't anyone minding the stand. Finally, a man emerged from the back room. "Forgive me," he said. "I can't hear a thing when I'm out back. Can I help you?"

Lizzie stared at him. It was the cranky

know-it-all man from the horse show, Mr. Bixby! For a moment, she forgot why she was even there. Then she caught herself. "Can you tell me which apples are good for cooking?" she asked. "I'm making apple butter."

Just then, Mrs. Bixby appeared from outside, dusting off her hands. "Hal, you didn't tell me we had customers," she said. "If you're making apple butter, I'd go with the Braeburn or the Cortland. Or a mixture." She pointed to two baskets that were next to each other.

"Thanks," said Lizzie. She filled two bags quickly. Kathy was waiting with a trailer full of horses, and Maria stood out in front of the farm stand, holding Barney on his leash. Who knew when he would start barking again?

The next time Lizzie glanced up, she realized that both Mr. and Mrs. Bixby were staring at Barney.

The pup sat in the grass, basking in a ray of

sunlight. He cocked his head to one side, listening. His caramel coat gleamed like a brand-new penny. He really was the cutest puppy. Then Barney's ears perked up.

Yip, yip, yip! Barney yanked his leash right out of Maria's hand. He ran to a tree, put his paws on its trunk, and barked up at a squirrel.

Maria rushed over to the pup and grabbed the leash. Barney kept barking. "Yeah, I see that squirrel, Barney," she said. "Good job, Barney." She pulled him back to the trailer.

Lizzie braced herself for a grumpy comment from Mr. Bixby. "Cute dog" was all he said.

"Yes," Lizzie said. "But he's not mine. I'm just, um, watching him." She didn't want to get into the whole story.

Mrs. Bixby weighed the apples and added up some numbers on a paper bag. "We saw you at the horse show. Isn't that Kathy's trailer?" She showed Lizzie the total she owed. "We know Kathy. She's a good neighbor."

"Cool," said Lizzie. "She's my friend's riding instructor. She's driving us home." Lizzie handed her money to Mrs. Bixby and held out her hand for change. She wanted to get out of there before Mr. Bixby said anything mean about Barney.

"That puppy is very lively," Mrs. Bixby said, counting out Lizzie's change. "He has a mind of his own, I gather."

"Yup," Lizzie said. Was she ever going to get out of there?

"Typical dachshund," Mr. Bixby said, in that gruff voice of his.

Lizzie shuffled her feet as she waited for Mrs. Bixby to give her the change.

"I hope the apple butter turns out well, dear," Mrs. Bixby said as she finally handed it over.

"Thanks." Lizzie pocketed her money. "Have a

good day." Lizzie jogged toward the truck with the heavy bags of apples in her arms. When she looked back, both Mr. and Mrs. Bixby were waving.

Lizzie was relieved to get out of there. Mrs. Bixby was nice, but Mr. Bixby sure was grumpy. It wasn't until Kathy had driven a few miles down the road that Lizzie remembered. She had forgotten to buy the doughnuts.

CHAPTER SIX

"But I love apple-cider doughnuts," Charles said, for the fifteenth time after dinner that night. "How could you forget them?"

"I told you, Barney distracted me," Lizzie said. "He was barking, and I thought the farm stand owners were going to get mad at him."

Charles rolled his eyes. "That's not a very good excuse."

"I know," said Lizzie. "I'm sorry, okay?" She was exhausted. It had been a long day, and Barney had not calmed down when she'd gotten him home.

As soon as he had arrived, Barney had acted like the boss of everyone. Even though he was smaller than Buddy, he tried to steal all Buddy's toys. As soon as he discovered the backyard, Barney wanted to go outside—and then come back inside—every five minutes. And he begged for attention constantly, putting his tiny paws up on Lizzie's legs and barking if she ignored him.

"I'm sorry, Mom," Lizzie said as she let Barney out for the tenth time. She could tell her mom was not enjoying Barney's antics.

Mom patted her shoulder. "It's okay," she said. "We've had wild puppies before. We'll manage— as long as he's not here too long. Anyway, dinner's almost ready. Can you set the table?"

By the time Lizzie and her family sat down to eat, Barney had cuddled up close to Buddy. They were both sound asleep on Buddy's bed in the living room. Barney had his front paws tucked under his chin. He was so sweet and peaceful when he was asleep.

After dinner, Lizzie headed upstairs to use Mom's computer to do a little more research on wirehaired dachshunds. Maybe she could learn more about the best ways to train a wild child like Barney.

It was almost bedtime when the phone rang. "It's for you," Dad said, handing her the phone. "It's Polly, Barney's owner." He raised his eyebrows.

"Hello?" Lizzie said. She felt a knot in her stomach. She guessed she knew what Polly was going to say. It didn't take her long to get to the point.

"We love Barney, but he makes things very hard, especially with Cassie," Polly said. "They get into trouble together all the time. I worry that one of these days he'll lose patience with her rough handling. I can already tell, just from a few hours without him here, how much more peaceful our lives are Barney deserves a loving home. I wish it could be ours—but I see now that it can't."

Polly sounded upset. Lizzie knew Mavis and Cassie had to be sad, too. "Maybe I can find him a new home that's close by," Lizzie suggested. "Then you and Mavis and Cassie could visit him sometimes."

"Wow," Polly said. "That would be amazing."

Lizzie promised to do her best. Barney was so cute and sweet. How hard could it be to find him a new home?

After breakfast that morning, Charles and the Bean took Buddy outside for a little playtime without Barney bothering him, while Lizzie and her parents talked about Polly's decision. Barney watched Buddy and Charles from the sliding door, barking and scrabbling at the glass, but Lizzie tried to ignore him.

Lizzie was still surprised that Polly had made up her mind so quickly. "Polly said it made a big difference to have Barney out of the house," she told her parents. "She made dinner, cleaned the kitchen, and packed all their bags for their trip. All because Barney wasn't there, causing more work for her."

"I can imagine," Mom said, rolling her eyes.

"It was nice—" Dad paused and waited for a break in Barney's barking. "It was nice of her to let us know so soon. Now you can start trying to find him a new home right away."

"Finding him the right place won't be easy. Any ideas?" Mom asked. "I have some tight deadlines this week, and I really can't think when he goes on like this." Mom was a reporter for the local newspaper, and she needed quiet in the house when she had a big story to write.

"I'll work on it. And I'm sure he'll settle down a little once he gets used to being here," said Lizzie. They all looked over at Barney, who still had his front paws propped up on the sliding door. He was barking nonstop at everything he saw.

It's a bird! It's a cloud! It's a leaf!

Lizzie gulped. Barney had been noisy at the horse show, but his bark was even louder in the house. He barked when someone came into the room. He barked when someone left the room. He barked when something passed by the window—a squirrel, a car, or a person pushing a stroller. What would he do if someone actually came to the front door?

Barney ran over to Lizzie and barked again, even more loudly. He put his paws up on her leg. She sighed and shook her head. Despite everything, he really was a cutie. Everybody thought she was so lucky because her family fostered dogs—but sometimes, it wasn't so easy.

CHAPTER SEVEN

After school on Monday, Maria walked home with Lizzie. "Thanks for helping me with the apple butter," Lizzie said.

"Of course," Maria said. "And you're going to help me with my tortillas on Wednesday, right?"

"Of course," Lizzie replied. "I just can't stay too late because I have to help out with Barney."

"I can't believe they're giving him up," Maria said, shaking her head.

"I know," Lizzie agreed. "But I understand why."

"Really?" Maria seemed surprised.

"Really. You'll understand, too," Lizzie told her friend as they neared her house. By the time they reached the mailbox, they could hear the barking.

Lizzie opened the front door, and both Barney and Buddy charged down the hall to run circles around Lizzie and Maria. "Hi, puppies," Lizzie called out over the yips and yaps. "Did you guys have fun today?"

"My guess is yes," Maria said, looking at the puppies' happy faces. "They're—um—excited."

"I know," said Lizzie. "I think Barney is always excited. He just never stops."

Maria knelt down, too. She scratched Barney behind the ears.

"Barney sure does have plenty of energy," Mom said. She and the Bean were in the living room, playing with his train set. "He ran circles around Buddy all day."

"Circles!" the Bean said. He stood up and spun around until he fell.

"He's wearing us all out," Mom said, laughing at the Bean. "And it hasn't always been easy keeping the Bean away from him. But I have to admit Barney was helpful today. I was in the basement doing laundry, and I heard this weird bark, almost a howl. When I came to check on him, the UPS deliveryman was at the door. I just hadn't heard the doorbell."

"Well, that's good to hear. At least you can be handy. Right, boy?" Lizzie rubbed Barney's belly. "Maria and I will play with him while we're waiting for the apple butter to cook down," said Lizzie. "We can take turns stirring."

"Sounds good," Mom said. "I'll help you get started."

Buddy had settled down next to the Bean, but Barney followed Lizzie and Maria and Mom into the kitchen.

"I printed out the recipe," Mom said, placing it on the counter. "It isn't hard. It just takes a lot of time to peel all the apples. Once they're cooking, the main thing is to keep stirring so the mixture doesn't burn on the bottom."

Barney "helped" while Maria and Lizzie got ready to cook. He barked when they opened drawers. He barked when they opened cupboards. And he barked when they opened the fridge.

What are you doing? It can't be more important than playing with me.

Just as they started washing the apples, the Bean trotted into the kitchen. "Barney!" he called out. He barreled toward the puppy with open arms.

Lizzie was about to grab the Bean, but Barney took matters into his own paws. He put his ears back and scampered away as quickly as he could. He tucked his tail between his short legs and scooted right out of the kitchen.

"I don't think Barney wants to play right now," Mom said to the Bean. "Why don't we go read a book?" She gave Lizzie a look, and Lizzie knew just what it meant: find that puppy a home, *fast*.

Soon after Mom and the Bean left, Barney returned. He walked over to the back door and sat down, barking.

"Do you want to go outside?" Lizzie asked. When she opened the door, the little dog bounded out and dashed around the yard, barking madly.

Lizzie had only peeled two apples when she heard Barney at the door. He scrabbled at the glass, wagging his little tail at high speed. He looked proud of himself.

"That was fast," Lizzie said as she slid open the door. Barney bolted inside, leaving muddy paw prints with every step. "Slow down, Barney," Lizzie called out. "I have to clean your paws." She reached for the old towel they kept by the door.

"I can hold him," Maria offered.

"Be careful," Lizzie said. "You have to cradle him and support him the right way. Dachshunds can have back problems since their backs are so long." She showed Maria how to hold Barney, then carefully went to work with the towel. Barney licked Maria's hands while Lizzie wiped his feet. "You are such a good boy," Lizzie told him as she cleaned him up. When she was done, she scratched him behind the ears. "There you go."

When Maria put him down, Barney trotted into the living room and curled up for a nap next to Buddy.

"He's a handful, but he sure is cute," Maria said, watching him go. "I'll bet you can find that sweetie a new home in no time."

"He is pretty sweet," Lizzie agreed as she went to put the towel back and make sure the sliding door was closed. "Oh, no!" she said, looking out the window.

The backyard was dotted with holes. No wonder his paws were muddy—Barney had been digging again. Lizzie sighed. She would have to fill in the holes after they'd finished the apple butter. Barney had been outside less than ten minutes. How could he dig all those holes in such a short time? That was one fast pup.

The apple butter was not fast. It was slow. Lizzie and Maria had to core and peel all the apples, and then they had to cook the apple slices at low heat with sugar and spices. "I think my arm's about to fall off," Lizzie said after ten minutes of constant stirring.

"I can take a turn," Maria offered. Lizzie handed her the wooden spoon.

While Maria stirred, Lizzie cleaned up the kitchen.

"How are you going to find Barney a home?" Maria asked.

"I'll start by asking our vet if she knows any-one," Lizzie said as she tossed apple peels into the compost. "And I'll ask Ms. Dobbins, too. Maybe someone has asked for a small dog at Caring Paws." Caring Paws was the animal shelter where Lizzie volunteered. Ms. Dobbins was the director, and she often had good advice about foster puppies.

"Why not call now?" Maria said.

Lizzie jumped at the chance. "You're right. It's the perfect time. Barney is asleep, so I can actu-ally talk," she said. It was hard to concentrate when Barney was barking.

Dr. Gibson, the vet, picked up the phone right away. Lizzie told her about Barney. "He's so, so cute," Lizzie said. "His other family just wasn't right for him." She paused, trying to decide how to explain Barney. "He needs a little more attention than a busy family with two kids can give him."

When Lizzie hung up, she smiled at Maria. "She gave me three names!" Lizzie held the list up and waved it around.

Maria stared at her. "A little more attention?" she asked. "From what I saw, Cassie gave him *a lot* of attention. Wasn't that part of the problem?"

Lizzie sighed. "I guess I could have been a little more honest about Barney," Lizzie admitted.

"You think?" Maria asked.

"I'll tell Ms. Dobbins the truth," Lizzie promised.

Ms. Dobbins made it easy. She was always thinking about matching dogs and families, so she knew which were the right questions to ask.

Unfortunately, once Lizzie had told her all about Barney—the whole truth—Ms. Dobbins said she didn't know anyone who would be a good fit.

Lizzie frowned as she hung up the phone. "At least we have three names," Lizzie said to Maria. "I'll make the calls tonight. Maybe one of these will be Barney's forever home."

"Fingers crossed," Maria said. "But speaking of fingers, mine are cramped from all this stirring. It's your turn." She handed Lizzie the spoon.

CHAPTER EIGHT

Lizzie made the calls that night after dinner, but nobody answered. Disappointed, she left a short message at each number. When she arrived home from school the next day, Mom had great news for her. One of the people had called back.

"Her name is Diane Coleman, and she sounded perfect," said Mom.

Lizzie wondered. She knew from experience that "perfect" people did not always work out. "Did you tell her all the Barney facts?" Lizzie asked. Before bedtime the night before, Lizzie had made a list of all the important information about Barney—his good and bad points.

"I did," Mom said. "I read them right off your checklist."

"You told her he barks a lot?" Lizzie asked.

"Yes, I did. She said that when she was a kid she had a beagle who barked all the time, so that didn't really upset her," Mom said. "She recently started working from home, so she wants a dog for company."

"She sounds pretty good," Lizzie said. "Doesn't she, boy?" Lizzie knelt down and scratched Barney under his chin. He sniffed her hands with his chilly black nose, waggled his eyebrows at her, and pawed at her leg.

"Diane said she'll be home all afternoon. She lives on Oak Lane. That's not far at all. You and Barney could walk there," Mom suggested.

"You want to go for a walk, Barney?" Lizzie asked.

Barney's dark eyes sparkled and he ran circles

around Lizzie's legs. His tiny black toenails clattered against the wood floor.

Yes! Yes! A walk! I've been cooped up all day. I only got to go outside five or six or ten times!

Lizzie looked at his sweet face and smiled. Was she about to walk this puppy to his forever home?

She snapped the leash onto Barney's collar and hurried out the door.

Barney was thrilled to be outside. He trotted eagerly along the sidewalk, sniffing at everything. His tail swung back and forth in time. Even his long, silky ears seemed perky, bobbing on either side of his head like a toddler's pigtails. Twice, people walking by asked if they could pet him. Barney seemed to love meeting new people. "You're a star," Lizzie told him.

When they arrived at the address, Lizzie looked

the place over. Diane lived in the last house on a dead-end street. "It *is* perfect," Lizzie said. The fenced backyard was far enough from the other houses so his barking would not upset the neighbors.

"What do you think, boy?" Lizzie asked, smiling down at Barney. The puppy gazed up at her and yipped. Then he charged ahead, yanking on the leash.

"All right, I get it," Lizzie said, heading up the front walk. "Let's go meet her."

Lizzie rang the doorbell. She heard footsteps right away. Lizzie felt a flutter of hope rise in her chest.

When the door opened, Diane's big smile was the first thing Lizzie saw. Diane's very pregnant belly was the second.

"Hi," Lizzie said, trying to hide her surprise. "I'm Lizzie."

"Hi, I'm Diane," the woman said, reaching out her hand.

Lizzie shook Diane's hand, trying not to stare at her round belly.

"And *you* must be Barney." Diane got down on her knees and put out her hand. Barney smothered her hand in kisses.

"Hello, hello," Diane said, leaning in for a kiss. "You are the absolute cutest. It's so nice to meet you, Barney."

Lizzie bit her lip. She could tell that Diane and Barney got along. "He really likes you," Lizzie said.

"And I really like him," Diane said. "Your mom warned me that he barks all the time, but that's not a problem. I'm sure we can work on that."

Lizzie gulped. She already knew that Barney wasn't the right puppy for Diane—but how was she going to tell her that? "He does bark a lot," Lizzie said. "And he needs a lot of attention."

"Not a problem," Diane said again, scratching Barney's back. Barney rolled over, begging her to rub his soft, caramel-colored stomach.

Lizzie took a deep breath. "Maybe not. But— the truth is, Barney isn't a great puppy for a family with little kids," Lizzie said. "His previous family had a toddler, and it wasn't a good fit."

"Oh? Why not?" Diane asked.

"The little girl wanted to pick him up all the time, and he didn't like it," Lizzie explained. "Barney totally steers clear of my little brother, too. It's just as well, because if he felt threatened he might get nippy. Dachshunds can be that way."

Diane sat back on her heels. "Really?" she said. "Because—well, I'm pregnant."

Lizzie smiled. "I kind of noticed that."

"Maybe we could train Barney," Diane suggested. "I'm not due for six weeks. I have time. And the baby wouldn't even be crawling for at least six months." Diane looked up at Lizzie while she stroked Barney's tummy.

Lizzie hated to disappoint Diana, but she had to be honest. "I don't think it's a chance you want to take," she said. "I know people who have had puppies and babies at the same time. It's a lot of work, even with a dog who is good with young kids." Was Diane even listening? She just kept petting Barney.

Finally, Lizzie decided she just had to come out and say it. "I have to be fair to Barney, too," she blurted. "I think he would be happier with a different family."

Diane's face fell. "I get it," she said, giving Barney one more pat. "I'm sure you're right, but he sure is cute. I hope he finds the home he deserves."

On the walk home, Barney lagged instead of trotting, and he didn't seem as interested in sniffing every bush and tree. As soon as Lizzie got him inside and took off his leash, he flopped down under the coffee table. "It's okay, Barney," Lizzie said, rubbing him behind his silky ears. "There has to be a home that's right for you. Don't worry, boy."

Barney stared at Lizzie. Then he put his head down on his paws and let out a long sigh. Lizzie's parents wanted her to find Barney a new home as soon as she could. She had a feeling that Barney wanted that, too.

CHAPTER NINE

The next day, Lizzie went to Maria's after school. The World Food Fair was a day away, and Maria had to make enough tortillas—and fillings—for all the kids, plus teachers and staff.

"What kind of fillings are we making?" Lizzie asked as they washed their hands in the kitchen.

Lizzie loved eating over at Maria's house, especially on taco night. There were always lots of fillings and sauces. It was hard to choose, so Lizzie tried a little of everything, stuffing her tacos as full as she could.

"Mom said I should just bring beans, cheese, and one sauce. Otherwise, it will be too messy,"

Maria explained. She tied an apron around her waist. "We should get started. It's not hard to make tortillas, but it can take a lot of time."

Lizzie and Maria mixed the ingredients, then rolled the dough into balls.

"Now what?" Lizzie asked.

"Now we press them," said Maria. She put one of the balls onto the bottom plate of a metal press.

Lizzie pushed down on the handle of the press.

"Just a little harder," Maria said. "They have to be thin or the tortillas will be too chewy."

"Um, how many of these are we making?" Lizzie asked.

"We need three hundred, but we'll cut them in half. So a hundred and fifty," Maria answered cheerfully.

Lizzie groaned. This was going to take a while. Next time she ate Maria's mom's homemade tortillas, she would know how much work they took.

Lizzie thought her arms had gotten tired from stirring apple butter, but that was nothing compared to how they felt after pressing two dozen tortillas. "Look at my bicep!" Lizzie said, pointing at her arm muscle. "I'm pumped."

Maria laughed.

While they worked, Maria asked about Barney. Lizzie gave her the update. She hadn't heard back from two of the possible families, but she was still hoping that one was right for the wirehaired dachshund.

When Lizzie arrived home she was tired and ready for a rest, but first she took Barney out in the yard. Barney zipped around, barking at everything and nothing. Lizzie laughed, forgetting her tiredness as she watched the happy puppy play. Barney really was a special little guy.

When she came back in, Dad stopped her in the kitchen. "You got another phone call about Barney," he said. "From a guy named Neal? I was out in the garage and didn't have the list of Barney facts with me, so I told him you would call back."

"Thanks, Dad," Lizzie said. "Wish me luck."

Lizzie dialed the number. "Hello, I'd like to speak to Neal," she said.

"This is Neal," answered the voice on the other end.

He didn't sound like a little kid, but he was definitely not an adult, either. "Hi. This is Lizzie Peterson. Did you call about Barney, the wirehaired dachshund we're fostering?"

"Yup," the boy answered. "I was calling for my family. We're very interested in Barney."

"That's good to hear," Lizzie said. She felt hope

rising in her chest, but first she had to find out more. "Can I ask you some questions? Barney is a very special dog, and I want to make sure your family is a good fit. It's important to check on a few things before you even meet him."

"Sure," said Neal. "Ask away."

Lizzie asked a lot of questions and Neal gave her a lot of answers. Neal and his twin sister were sixteen. Everyone in the family loved dogs, and no one had allergies. They'd had a Maltese named Gigi who had died a few months ago. They did not mind barking.

"Is someone home during the day?" Lizzie asked, looking down at her checklist. She knew Barney was not a dog who could be alone all day while people were at work.

"Yup," Neal said. "My parents both work from home."

"Sounds great," Lizzie said, making a note on

her list. "And, let's see. Last but not least, do you have a fenced-in outdoor space?"

Neal paused. "Not really," he replied. "We live in an apartment. We didn't really need a yard for Gigi. We took her on walks and sometimes to the dog park."

Lizzie took a breath and told herself to be honest. The truth was important. She wanted to find the right home for Barney.

"Hello?" Neal said.

"Hi," Lizzie replied with a sigh. "I know some dogs are fine without a yard, but I'm pretty sure Barney would not be. He has lots of energy, and he wants to go in and out all the time."

Now Neal was quiet.

"And Barney really does bark a lot. Like, constantly. It might be too much in an apartment," she added. "You'd probably get complaints from the neighbors."

"He really barks that much?" Neal asked. "I guess that might be a problem while my parents are trying to work during the day. I hadn't thought about that."

Lizzie felt bad when she hung up. Neal had sounded so disappointed. Lizzie hated to say no, especially when it came to dogs. But Barney wasn't just any dog. She told herself that she had done the right thing. But where, oh where, was she going to find the perfect home for Barney?

CHAPTER TEN

Lizzie and Maria's stations were right next to each other for the World Food Fair. They had a prime spot, just outside the cafeteria. All day long, Maria had a crowd of kids waiting in line for tortillas, even though there was a lot of other food at the fair. Kids had brought everything from mini egg rolls and Italian flatbread to kimchi and Wisconsin cheese.

Lizzie had brought her apple butter in a slow cooker, and it filled the room with the smell of warm cinnamon. It also covered the table with sticky drips of cooked apples and sugar.

"What you need is someone who doesn't mind

the barking," Maria said. They'd been discussing the Barney Problem all afternoon.

Lizzie had talked to the third person on Dr. Gibson's list that morning before school, and she'd had to check them off, too. The family lived over two hours away, too far for Polly, Mavis, and Cassie to visit. Now, in the middle of World Food Fair day, the two friends were still trying to think of another solution.

"Maybe for the right people, the barking could even be good," Maria continued. "Like if they needed a watchdog."

Lizzie stared at her friend as a blob of apple butter dripped down her thumb. "What did you say?"

"I don't know," Maria said. "I was just brainstorming. A watchdog? Is that what I said?"

"Maria, you are brilliant!" Lizzie threw her arms around her friend.

"Yeah, right?" a kid with a mouthful of tortilla said. "She really is. These tacos are delicious."

"And you're such a good friend, too," Lizzie said, wiping her hand on her apron. "That's why I know you'll do me a big favor."

"A favor?" Maria asked.

"I need you to talk with Kathy," Lizzie said. "I've got a plan, and that's the first step."

"That's easy," said Maria. "I have my lesson today. But what's your plan?"

"It's so obvious," began Lizzie. For the rest of the school day, the two friends handed out food samples and talked about Lizzie's plan. It made so much sense. Lizzie didn't know why she hadn't thought of it before.

"I still don't get why you're insisting on getting apple-cider doughnuts today of all days," Mom said to Lizzie and Charles in the car later that day. "Didn't you just have the World Food Fair?"

"Yes, but you only get, like, one bite of all the stuff," Charles said. "And I've been craving dough-nuts ever since Lizzie forgot to bring them home."

"And besides, it's a good way to celebrate," Lizzie added. "You deserve a treat since you finished your article, Mom."

"I have a feeling you two are up to something," Mom said. "But a doughnut sounds yummy, and it's good to get the dogs out."

Barney and Buddy were in the backseat with Lizzie and Charles. Barney did not seem to bark as much when he was riding in the car. Lizzie stroked his long back. Barney was so easy to love—especially when he was being quiet.

Mom pulled into the grassy lot by the farm stand. Lizzie saw a familiar truck parked there.

"Isn't that Kathy's truck?" Mom asked.

"Yep," Lizzie said, jumping out. "Charles, you

keep Buddy." Lizzie took Barney's leash and hurried over to the truck.

Maria bounded out of the passenger side of Kathy's truck and gave Lizzie a hug. "Fingers crossed," she said as they headed toward the farm stand.

When Lizzie looked back, she saw Mom talking with Kathy. Kathy gave her a thumbs-up. "I guess it's all up to us now," she said, looking down at Barney.

With the others following behind, Lizzie and Maria and Barney approached the farm stand. Lizzie's heart was thumping. Once again, there wasn't anyone at the cash register. Before Lizzie could call out, Barney began to bark. He kept barking until Mrs. Bixby appeared from the back of the building, with Mr. Bixby right behind her.

"Hello," she called out. "Sorry you had to wait. I hate to make people wait." She made her way to the main table. "Well, hello, there!" She stooped over to give Barney a pat, and he grinned up at her, waggling his eyebrows.

"It's okay. We just got here," Maria told the couple.

"Still, I keep telling him we could use a bell or something." Mrs. Bixby stood up to give Mr. Bixby a knowing look.

Lizzie paused. "Actually, that's why we're here," she said.

"You want to sell us a bell?" Mr. Bixby asked, looking doubtful.

Lizzie smiled and shook her head. When she'd first seen him at the horse show, Lizzie had thought that Mr. Bixby was gruff and harsh, and kind of hard on Barney. He had very strong opinions. But as she'd learned more about dachshunds, she'd realized he might not be so mean after all. He really did know a lot about the breed, and maybe he was just thinking about what was best for Barney.

"I noticed that you know *a ton* about dachshunds," Lizzie began.

"We do," Mr. Bixby said. "Mrs. Bixby and I have had five dachshunds over the years. We just love them. They are terrific dogs."

"Well, we had this idea. We wanted to check with Kathy first, since she knows you. We didn't want to push anything on you, but Kathy—well, she thought you might be ready for another dog," said Lizzie. She glanced back at Kathy, and the trainer smiled and nodded.

"You mean this little sprite?" Mrs. Bixby asked, pointing at Barney. "The little troublemaker from the show?"

"Yes, he's looking for a new home," said Lizzie. "He might be small, but like most dachshunds, he's a lot of dog. Too much dog, for some. He needs just the right family." Lizzie pulled out her Barney checklist and went over the whole thing, spelling out all his good and bad points. She couldn't even look at the Bixbys while she read. This had to work!

When Lizzie was done, Mr. Bixby smiled. "You've pretty much nailed it with that list. Barney is a perfect example of a wirehaired dachshund." Lizzie thought she saw the hint of a smile.

"I don't mind barking," Mrs. Bixby said. "Goodness, my husband barks all the time. I think he and Barney have a lot in common."

Mr. Bixby and Barney both stared at Mrs. Bixby, and Lizzie had to laugh. They both wore the same expression, down to the wild eyebrows.

"They have a lot to say," Mrs. Bixby added, "and they both keep saying it until someone listens."

Lizzie coughed to hide another laugh.

"My wife might have a point," Mr. Bixby said.

This time, Lizzie was sure he was smiling. "Anyway, his barking wouldn't bug anyone around here." Mr. Bixby crouched down and put out his hand. Lizzie let go of the leash, and Barney made his way over to the older man. He sniffed his hands and licked his fingers.

"We live at the end of this road," Mrs. Bixby explained, pointing to the long, gravel lane. "Our house backs on a fenced orchard. There's no one else around for miles. He could bark, he could dig, he could run around outside all he wants."

"He wouldn't be bored. We're outside all the time: picking apples, pruning trees, working in the orchard," Mr. Bixby said. His long, thin fingers swept over Barney's back again and again.

"And I guess he would certainly help let us know when customers arrive at the farm stand!" Mrs. Bixby added.

Lizzie and Maria looked at each other,

grinning. "That's just what we were thinking," said Lizzie. "That's how we got the idea in the first place."

Lizzie had thought that she would have to convince the couple to adopt Barney. Now, Mr. and Mrs. Bixby were the ones trying to convince Lizzie.

"But what about Barney's other family?" asked Mrs. Bixby, frowning. "What about that cute little girl? She seemed to really love this pup. What happened to them?"

"They do love Barney, but they decided he wasn't the right dog for them right now," Lizzie said.

Mr. Bixby slowly nodded his head. Then he shook it ever so slightly. "From what I saw, I think that was the right decision," he said, looking at the ground. "Dachshunds and toddlers aren't always a good mix, and of course we would make sure that Barney didn't bother any of our younger customers. But I feel bad. Giving him up had to be hard. Especially for the little girl."

"Well, I know they would love to come visit him sometimes," Lizzie said. "If you would be okay with that."

"Of course," Mrs. Bixby said. "They can come by our house anytime. Or they can visit us here at the farm stand."

"We'll give them free doughnuts whenever they come," Mr. Bixby added. "Least we can do."

Charles had been standing nearby, holding Buddy's leash. Now he perked up. "Can we please get some doughnuts, too?" he asked. "I mean, now that everything's been decided about Barney's new forever home."

Everybody laughed.

Mr. Bixby looked at Lizzie, eyebrows raised. "*Has* it been decided?" he asked.

"I guess it has," Lizzie said. She felt tears pop into her eyes as she watched Mr. Bixby bend down to scoop Barney up into his arms.

"Let's celebrate!" Mrs. Bixby said. "Doughnuts for everyone, on the house."

Charles rushed forward, and Maria and Kathy followed him toward the doughnut case.

Lizzie hung back for a moment, watching Mrs. Bixby hand out doughnuts while Mr. Bixby held Barney, cradling him in his arms to support his back. Mom came over to give Lizzie a hug, and they both smiled as they saw the little pup lick the old man's face.

I have a feeling I'm going to be very happy here.

"Another puppy finds a forever home," said Mom, giving Lizzie a squeeze. "Barney wasn't easy, but I know you'll miss him."

"I sure will," said Lizzie. It was never easy saying good-bye to a foster puppy—even one as wild as Barney—but she was positive that she had found him the best possible home. She smiled up at her mom. "Now, let's go get our doughnuts!"

PUPPY TIPS

I love to hug my dog, Zipper—but did you know that some dogs really don't enjoy being hugged? If you pay attention to their body language, they'll let you know. If your dog pulls away, looks frightened or uncomfortable (ears back, whites of eyes showing, trembling, or panting are all signs), or even growls or shows her teeth, she might not like what you're doing. Of course, you should never hug a dog you don't know! It's better to start off by letting a new dog sniff your hand. Then you can pet the dog gently if the owner says it's okay.

Dear Reader,

I think wirehaired dachshunds are the cutest! I'm more
of a big-dog person, but if I were ever to get a little dog,
I would consider a dog like Barney. I used to know a
wirehaired dachshund named Simon, and he was like
a big dog in a little dog's body. He really did remind me
of a cartoon character the way he bounced around—
and I loved his funny, furry face! I think a dog like that
would keep me laughing every day.

For another book about a dachshund, try *Ziggy.* If you
like reading about horses, try *Rascal.* (That's the book
where Lizzie takes riding lessons with Kathy.) And if you
want to learn more about dog body language, you might
like *Rusty!*

Yours from the Puppy Place,
Ellen Miles

ABOUT THE AUTHOR

Ellen Miles loves dogs, which is why she has a great time writing the Puppy Place books. And guess what? She loves cats, too! (In fact, her very first pet was a beautiful tortoiseshell cat named Jenny.) That's why she came up with the Kitty Corner series. Ellen lives in Vermont and loves to be outdoors with her dog, Zipper, every day, walking, biking, skiing, or swimming, depending on the season. She also loves to read, cook, explore her beautiful state, play with dogs, and hang out with friends and family.

Visit Ellen at ellenmiles.net.